HOME

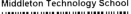

Titles in Teen Reads:

Copy Cat
TOMMY DONBAVAND

Fair Game
ALAN DURANT

Mama Barkfingers
CAVAN SCOTT

Dead Scared
TOMMY DONBAVAND

Jigsaw Lady
TONY LEE

Pest Control
CAVAN SCOTT

Just Bite
TOMMY DONBAVAND

Mister Scratch
TONY LEE

The Hunted
CAVAN SCOTT

Home
TOMMY DONBAVAND

Stalker
TONY LEE

The Changeling
CAVAN SCOTT

Kidnap
TOMMY DONBAVAND

Dawn of the Daves
TIM COLLINS

Nightmare
ANN EVANS

Ward 13
TOMMY DONBAVAND

Joke Shop
TIM COLLINS

Sitting Target
JOHN TOWNSEND

Deadly Mission
MARK WRIGHT

The Locals
TIM COLLINS

Snow White,
Black Heart
JACQUELINE RAYNER

Ghost Bell
MARK WRIGHT

Troll
TIM COLLINS

The Wishing Doll
BEVERLY SANFORD

The Corridor
MARK WRIGHT

Insectoids
ROGER HURN

Underworld
SIMON CHESHIRE

Death Road
JON MAYHEW

Billy Button
CAVAN SCOTT

World
Without Words
JONNY ZUCKER

Badger Publishing Limited, Oldmedow Road, Hardwick Industrial Estate, King's Lynn PE30 4JJ
Telephone: 01438 791037

www.badgerlearning.co.uk

HOME

TOMMY DONBAVAND

Home ISBN 978-1-78147-569-0

Text ©Tommy Donbavand 2014
Complete work © Badger Publishing Limited 2014

Publisher: Susan Ross
Senior Editor: Danny Pearson
Copyeditor: Cheryl Lanyon
Designer: Bigtop Design Ltd
Cover image: Kiselev Andrey Valerevich/Shutterstock.com

6 8 10 9 7

CHAPTER 1

FARTING

Like most of our family day trips, the last one we ever took ended in an argument.

"Mum!" moaned my big sister, Fiona, from the back seat of the car. "Max is farting again!"

My mum sighed from the front passenger seat. "Max, stop it!" she snapped. Beside her, my dad gripped the steering wheel tightly.

"I can't help it," groaned Max, clutching at his stomach. "I don't feel well."

"Then you should have had a proper breakfast instead of gobbling down a handful of biscuits just before we left."

Max turned to me and winked. He had complete control over his farts. It was his party trick. He can let one rip on demand – and he's really proud of the fact.

Even though we're identical twins, there are some big differences between me and Max. I'm into rugby, while he likes motorbikes. I can turn my eyelids inside out, and he can fart at will. I'd never told him, but I'd much prefer to have his disgusting skill.

I tried it once, during a science test at school. It didn't end well.

"Mum!" cried Fiona. "He's done it again!"

My mum twisted round in her seat to glare at Max. "Stop blowing off!"

"I told you," said Max as innocently as he could.

"I can't help it."

"Then swap places with Danny."

"No, we can't do that," I said, pushing myself out towards the edge of the seat. "I feel sick if I sit in the middle. I have to stay by the window."

"What, so I have to put up with his stink?" exclaimed Fiona.

"Language!" snapped my mum.

"But he smells!"

"Then wind your window down, Fiona. And stop going on. We'll be there soon."

Fiona slumped back in the seat, her arms folded. "I didn't want to go to a stupid castle in the first place," she muttered. "I was supposed to be going shopping with Kelly today."

My dad's fingers tightened around the leather cover of the steering wheel.

"You spend too much time with that girl," said my mum. "She's a bad influence."

"But she's only..."

"Seventeen is too young to get a tattoo, Fiona," interrupted my mum. "You are not getting one."

"But…"

"End of discussion!"

Fiona was really fuming now. It wouldn't take much to make her blow, big time, and I could feel Max squirming around in the seat between us, brewing up another bottom burp.

"Still no reason to be stomping around some windy old castle on a Saturday," grumbled Fiona. "It's like some sort of child cruelty, if you ask me."

I heard my dad grind his teeth.

"Harlech Castle is a fascinating place," said my mum, waving a tourist information leaflet in our direction. "Besides, Max and Danny have to choose a castle for their history project. Harlech is perfect for them."

"Yeah," said Max with a grin. "And you never know, Fiona, it might not be as windy as you think." Then he leaned against me, lifted his right buttock off the seat, and let one rip...

FART!

"You are disgusting!" screamed Fiona, punching Max repeatedly in the arm.

"Ow!" he shouted, almost crying with laughter. "That one wasn't me — it was Danny!"

"Don't blame me!" I yelled. "That was a Max Dunnock special!"

"I want to go home!" whined Fiona.

"ENOUGH!" roared my dad. He spun round in his seat and glared at the three of us. I felt Max shrink back beside me. He'd gone too far this time, and he knew it.

"I'm turning this car around right now!" barked my dad, "And when I get you three home…"

Suddenly, my mum screamed, "Phil, look out!"

My dad turned back just in time to see the cement lorry heading straight for us.

Then everything went black.

CHAPTER 2

WAKING

My eyes felt sticky when I tried to open them, like I'd been sleeping really heavily. I raised a hand to rub them, and heard a gasp.

A chair scraped back and someone dashed out of the room. There must have been another person there, though, because I heard water trickling, and then a damp cloth wiped my eyes.

One by one, my eyelids became unstuck, and I forced them open.

Everything was a blur, but I could make out enough to tell that I was in a room with white walls. The bedroom I share with my brother is painted blue, so that ruled that out.

I heard voices and turned to see people hurrying into the room. They were little more than out-of-focus shapes at first, but then the damp cloth was wiped across my eyes again and I found I could see my mum as she leaned over to hug me.

"Oh, Danny!" she cried. "You're back!"

Back? I hadn't been anywhere, had I?

Actually, looking around the room, I got the impression that I'd been here for quite a while. I was lying in a bed with cool, white sheets, and there were all sorts of computer monitors sitting beside me. Get-well cards were stuck to the wall behind me, and there was a bunch of flowers that was past its best sitting in a water jug near the window, a half-deflated helium balloon tied to the handle.

I was in hospital.

"Wha… wha…?" I said — or rather, I tried to say, but I could only make weird croaking sounds that hurt my throat.

A figure appeared beside my mum. It was my dad. His face was covered in sticking plasters. He had a black eye, and there were bruises stretching right across his forehead. He poured a glass of water (thankfully, not from the flower jug), and helped me to sit up and take a drink.

"What happened?" I whispered as I lay back down. My voice still wasn't back to normal.

"There was an accident," said my mum, clutching my hand. "In the car, on the way to Harlech Castle."

I blinked my sore eyes and tried to remember, but there was nothing there. "I… I don't…"

"It's OK," said my dad softly. "The doctors said it may not come back to you straight away. Not after everything you've been through."

"Everything I've been through?" I wheezed. "What do you mean?"

Tears were running down my mum's cheeks. "You've been in a coma, sweetheart."

"A... a coma?" My mind raced as I tried to remember something — anything — but it was empty, as though someone had completely wiped my memory.

"How long?"

It was Fiona who replied. "Two weeks," she said, approaching my bed. She looked shorter than usual, and then I realised she was sitting in a wheelchair. Her right leg was coated in a white plaster cast, and was sticking straight out ahead of her.

"What happened to you?" I asked.

"Broken leg," Fiona replied with a shrug. "Dislocated shoulder, too, but they popped that back into place almost as soon as we first arrived at the hospital."

I turned back to my mum and studied her for wounds. Her left wrist was bandaged and she had a gash running from just above her right eye back into her hair that had obviously needed stitches.

"You were very lucky, Danny," she said, gripping my hand even tighter than before. "A bang on the head that knocked you out, but that's all. We're just glad you're back with us now. We've missed you." She forced a smile, but I could tell there was sadness behind it.

And then it hit me. Someone was missing.

My eyes scanned the room, but he wasn't there.

"Where's Max?" I asked.

CHAPTER 3

RAINING

It rained the day of Max's funeral. I don't know if you've ever been to a funeral. If not, count yourself lucky. They're horrible. I'd been to a couple in the past — one for my grandad, and another for our elderly next-door neighbour. But this was worse than anything I ever could have expected.

Fourteen years Max and I had been together, with barely more than a day apart. He'd been born three minutes before me, which meant, according to him, that he always got to open his birthday presents first, and to blow out the first lot of candles on the cake.

The first time we'd ever been separated was when we were invited to Lenny Cook's sleepover when we were eight, but I couldn't go because I had chicken pox. Even then, we didn't last an entire night apart. Lenny's mum rang my mum at midnight to say that Max couldn't sleep without me and he wanted to come home. She drove all the way to get him in her pink Eeyore pyjamas.

She wasn't wearing pink today, though. She was in black, like everyone else. Fiona even had a black stocking pulled over the white plaster cast on her leg.

I stood at the edge of the grave and watched as my brother's coffin was lowered into the ground. It looked too small, somehow, almost as though he couldn't have fitted inside comfortably. I don't know why that bothered me — that he wouldn't be comfortable. Odd the kinds of things you think about at times like this.

My mum and dad had held off the funeral until I had woken up from my coma and was able to be there to say goodbye, even though they'd really had no idea how long it was going to be before I finally came round. I think they understood that I had to be here; that I wasn't just losing a brother, but also a part of myself.

I felt a hand clamp down on my rain-soaked shoulder and caught a whiff of whisky. I didn't have to turn around to know it was my dad. He'd been drinking a lot ever since the accident, according to Fiona. She said that our mum and dad had barely said two words to each other all the time I was unconscious.

I'd love to be able to tell him that the accident hadn't been his fault, but the truth was I still couldn't remember much about the event. Just flashes of images, as though I was looking through someone else's collection of photographs of the crash.

The priest said a few words as the coffin reached the bottom of the hole, rain spattering hard on its wooden surface. My own tears were mixed in with the raindrops as I took a last look down at Max's final resting place.

See you, buddy.

CHAPTER 4

KNOCKING

The next week was like hell. Everyone in the family was so quiet! Dad sat in the kitchen, working his way through one bottle of scotch after another, while my mum and Fiona took up camp in the living room, making pointless chatter with a steady stream of well-wishers we didn't want to see, and couldn't wait to get rid of. There were times when I wanted to scream — just to bring some sound of life back into the house — but, of course, I didn't.

I spent most of the week in the bedroom I used to share with Max. No, that's not right...

I spent most of the week on *my side* of the bedroom. I don't know why, but I stayed on *my* bed, read *my* comics, played *my* games and left all his stuff alone. We never really fought but, when we did, it was usually about one of us touching the other one's things without permission. One time, he accused me of stealing a tenner from his money box and threatened to move into the spare room where our mum kept all her boxes of craft supplies, but we both knew that would never happen.

"Thanks for coming. Bye!"

I sat on the top landing and waited until my mum had closed the door on yet another kind but time-consuming neighbour, then jogged down the stairs to the kitchen to get myself a can of cola. Dad was sitting at the end of the dining table, unshaven, his shirt unbuttoned, and a glass of whisky clamped in his hand. He was on his second bottle tonight already!

"You alright?" I asked as I pulled open the fridge door and grabbed my can.

He didn't reply.

"I think that was Mrs Grainger from number 32..."

"Bleedin' busybody!" my dad slurred before taking a gulp of the whisky. He winced as the stuff hit the back of his throat.

"Yeah..." I said in a half-hearted attempt at agreeing. "Can I get you anything?"

My dad shook his head.

"OK... I'll, er... leave you to it, then."

Without waiting for a reply, I made my exit into the living room. Fiona was lying on the sofa, her broken leg propped up on a pile of cushions, flicking through TV channels on the remote.

"What are you watching?" I asked, popping open my can with a hiss.

"Nothing, really," she said without looking up.

I turned to my mum. She was sitting in her usual chair, working on one of her craft kits — a latch hook rug set. I watched the needle dart in and out of the fabric, each stitch securing a length of brightly coloured wool in place.

I struggled to think of something to say to her. Anything at all! But everything I could think of sounded so stupid and useless and wrong. I sat in silence for a few minutes, until...

"I'll be up in my room."

I sprinted out of the living room, taking the stairs two at a time and slamming the bedroom door behind me. With trembling fingers, I dropped the can of cola onto the desk Max and I shared, slopping a puddle of brown liquid over an old motorbike magazine as I did so. He'd have gone mad at me for doing that, but now there was just silence.

Without warning, my eyes flooded with tears and I threw myself onto Max's bed, burying my face in his pillow and sobbing hard. I needed my brother, my best friend. There was no way I could go on like this for the rest of...

Knocking at the front door. Hammering almost. Another bloody visitor!

"I'll get it," I heard my mum say to Fiona, downstairs. "You stay there and rest your leg."

No, I decided. No more nosy neighbours turning up with a lukewarm casserole and an appetite for gossip. *Did you hear about the Dunnocks? About the accident? They say their boy Max didn't have his seatbelt fastened properly. That he went right through the windscreen. Mind you, I blame the father. Always been a heavy drinker, that one. I'll bet he was drunk when he crashed the car that day.*

No more! Wiping my tears, I raced out of the room and down the stairs to get to the door before my mum. Whoever was outside was determined to get our attention. They were still knocking, as loudly as ever.

I twisted the handle and yanked the door open as hard as I could.

"Can't you just leave us alo… "

The words stuck in my throat and I felt my heart pound in my chest. The world around me began to swim out of focus.

Standing on the doorstep was my twin brother, Max.

CHAPTER 5

HUGGING

I stared at the figure on the doorstep.

"M... Max?" I whispered.

The figure took an awkward step towards me. It looked like Max — but like Max with pale, damp skin. He was wearing his smart blue suit — the one we'd both been bought for Uncle Bernard's wedding last year.

The suit he'd been buried in.

Max's mouth began to open and close, but no sound came out. I stared at his pale blue lips and struggled to work out what he was trying to say. Maybe I was just wishing it to be true, but it looked as though he was mouthing the word 'Danny' over and over.

I heard a gasp behind me and turned to see my mum in the doorway of the living room. She was clinging to the doorframe and shaking.

"Max!" she cried. "Phil! Come quickly! Our baby boy has come home!"

Fiona appeared beside her, hobbling on her plaster cast. "It can't be true!"

"It is!" I said, tears running down my cheeks again. "He's home!"

I stepped out into the cold night air and carefully took my brother by the arm, helping him to shuffle over the step and into the house. Max looked at me and smiled. He took small, awkward steps as though the muscles in his legs were refusing to cooperate.

As I closed the front door, my mum raced over and flung her arms around my twin, hugging him tightly. This must have squeezed the air out of his lungs as Max finally spoke out loud.

"... missed you..."

"Oh, and we missed you, too!" sobbed my mum.

I wrapped my arms around my mum and Max and, after a few awkward hops along the hallway, so did Fiona. The four of us just stood there, not saying anything. Just hugging.

Eventually, we helped Max down to the living room and gently lowered him into the space Fiona had been taking up on the sofa. He lay awkwardly, his arms and legs rigid.

Beneath the soft glow of the lamp in the corner, my brother's face looked as though it was made of wax, and his eyes were little more than dark holes which darted from side to side, as though taking everything in for the first time.

My mum sat on the edge of the sofa and took Max's hand in hers. She examined his fingertips and found them full of dark splinters. Max must have clawed his way out of his coffin with his bare hands!

"Danny, get my sewing kit."

I grabbed a small box from beside my mum's armchair and passed it over. She found a pair of tweezers and began to pluck the splinters from his flesh, one by one.

"Sorry if this hurts a bit," my mum said.

Max pressed against his chest again, forcing air across his vocal chords. "No... feeling..."

My mum smiled. "Well, at least there's one advantage to being..." her voice trailed away before she reached the end of the sentence. She worked with the tweezers in silence for a while, then spoke again.

"They told us you were dead, Max. The doctors in the hospital, I mean."

Max nodded. "Dead... yes..."

"Then, how have you done this?"

"Don't... know...," Max wheezed. "Was scared... wished... for home... woke up... dark..."

"Well, you don't have to be scared any more, sweetheart," said my mum as she leaned over to kiss Max on the forehead. "Ooh, you're freezing cold. I'll nip up and run you a nice hot bath."

My mum hurried out of the room and everything fell quiet. I glanced over at Fiona, and she lookcd back at me. I could tell we were both nervous about talking to our own brother, but that was stupid. He was just Max, the twin I'd grown up with. The trouble was that I couldn't think of anything to say to him after what had happened.

Max turned his head towards me and began to press down on his chest again. "You'd... better not... have... touched... any of... my stuff..."

I grinned. That was better. That was just like Max again.

I hurried over and sat on the floor next to the sofa. "What was it like?" I asked. "Being dead?"

"Danny, don't!" Fiona cried, covering her ears with her hands.

But I wanted to know. "When I was in my coma, there was nothing. Just blackness," I explained. "Just the crash, then waking somewhere else..."

"Same... for me..." said Max. "Except... there was..."

He stopped speaking and his eyes flickered upwards as a shadow fell over us both.

"Move away, Danny!" growled a voice.

CHAPTER 6

THREATENING

I turned to see my dad standing in the living room doorway. His eyes were bloodshot and he was swaying from side to side. He took a step into the room and I jumped to my feet when I realised that he was holding a kitchen knife in his hand.

"What's that monster doing here?"

"That's not a monster, Dad," said Fiona. "It's Max. He's come home."

My dad shook his head. "Max is dead. I killed him."

On the sofa, Max shook his head. "No..." he hissed. "Accident..."

"Accident or not, you're supposed to be six feet underground." My dad took another drunken step towards Max.

I blocked his way. "Leave him alone, Dad. He's your son."

My dad shook his head. "He's a zombie."

Zombie! The word caught me off guard and echoed around my head. My brother wasn't a zombie! OK, he had died, been buried, then reanimated and climbed out of his grave...

Oh, dear God! Max was a zombie!

"I don't care!" I said, glancing back at my twin. "I won't let you hurt him."

"I can't hurt him!" bellowed my dad. "He's dead! It's *him* that'll hurt us! Come on, Danny! We've watched enough zombie films to know what happens next. One bite and we'll be shuffling around hungry for brains, just like him!"

"Not... like that..." croaked Max. "Don't... want... brains..."

My dad waved the knife in Max's direction. "I don't need your opinion!" he spat. "**And** I can't let you stay like this. You'll kill us all."

"So, what are you going to do?" I demanded. "Cut his head off or something?"

"That's what they tell you to do in the films..."

"But that's made up!" cried Fiona. "This is real!"

"Which is exactly why I have to do it," growled my dad. He made to push past me, but I pressed a hand to his chest to stop him.

"You'll have to go through me, first," I said flatly.

"And me," added Fiona, hobbling over to stand with me.

My dad glared down at us, the whisky fumes on his breath stinging my eyes. "You two haven't got the strength to stop me!" he snarled.

"No, but I have!" said a voice. My dad had started to turn round to see who had spoken, when my mum punched him hard in the face. And I mean really hard! I heard the CRACK! as his nose broke from the blow, blood spraying across the carpet.

"You stupid woman!" my dad roared, dropping the kitchen knife so that he could clamp his hands to his face. "He's a zombie! He'll kill all of us!"

"No, not all of us," said my mum, surprisingly calmly. "Because not all of us live here any more..."

Fiona and I shared a glance as the full impact of her words sunk home.

My mum strode to the front door and opened it. "Get out," she said to my dad. "Now."

His hands still pressed to his broken nose, my dad looked from me to Fiona, and then down at Max on the sofa. Then he left without saying another word, pushing past my mum and staggering out into the night air.

I hurried down the hall to hug my mum. "Are you OK?" I asked.

She nodded. "I'll be fine," she said. "We'll all be fine. There's nothing to worry about any more."

And then a police car pulled up at the end of our driveway.

CHAPTER 7

HIDING

"Quick!" hissed my mum, shutting the front door. "Fiona, get Max upstairs to the bathroom and lock yourselves in. Danny, wipe the blood off the living room carpet!"

We ran to our tasks. Fiona pulled Max to his feet and dragged him up the stairs one at a time. With her leg in the cast and Max's awkward walk, they looked like a comedy act, but I didn't have time to laugh. I raced into the kitchen, grabbed a tea towel and ran it under the tap.

DING DONG!

The doorbell rang.

I ran back into the living room, dropped to my knees and started to mop up my dad's blood. But it just smeared. The more I scrubbed, the more the stain spread. I was making it worse!

I heard my mum answer the front door. "Oh, hello, Sergeant Todd. I wasn't expecting to see you this evening." Perfect! Sergeant Todd was the police officer who had questioned us about the car accident. He'd even been to Max's funeral. What was he going to make of all this?

"No, of course it's not too late," I heard my mum say. "Come on through..."

I had to hide the blood! Jumping up, I grabbed the first thing I could find — my mum's half-finished rug kit — and dropped it over the stain on the carpet. Then I stuffed the blood-soaked tea towel into my pocket and dropped to the floor...

...just as Sergeant Todd walked into the room.

"Evening, Danny," he said, taking off his hat. "Sorry to disturb you all so late."

"That's OK," I said with a shrug. "I was just, er... helping my mum work out where this rug will go when she's finished it."

The police officer glanced down at the half rug I was lying on. "It looks very nice," he said. My mum came into the room behind him.

"Is your husband at home, Mrs Dunnock?" Sergeant Todd asked. "I was hoping to talk to the whole family."

"No," said my mum. "Phil's had to go away for work suddenly."

"And young Fiona?"

"She's in the bath, I think," I said as innocently as I could.

"OK," said the police officer, sitting on the edge of the sofa. "I'm afraid I have some rather upsetting news. Danny, do you want to sit down so I can talk to you and your mum?"

"No," I said, spotting the kitchen knife lying near the policeman's foot. I stretched out my arm to cover it. "I'm fine here."

"Danny really likes my rugs!" said my mum with an over-eager smile.

Sergeant Todd nodded, then got down to business. "I'm sorry to tell you that Max's grave has been vandalised."

"Vandalised?" said my mum. "How?"

The sergeant sighed. "It has been dug up, Mrs Dunnock, and the coffin has been broken into." He took another deep breath. "There's no easy way to tell you this, but whoever desecrated the grave has also taken Max's body."

"My little boy has gone?" cried my mum. She buried her face in her hands and started to sob. I had no idea she was such a good actress!

My mum and I sat there (well, I lay there) for the next fifteen minutes, pretending to cry and listening to Sergeant Todd explain how the police were already out looking for the body snatcher and how they would leave no stone unturned until they found Max.

Eventually, my mum stood up and shook the policeman's hand. "Thank you for letting us know," she said, wiping away her fake tears. "Danny, would you like to show Sergeant Todd to the door?"

I flicked my eyes down to the patch of carpet I was lying on. My muscles were beginning to stiffen up. "No," I said. "Not really. Very comfortable here..."

"Oh, of course!" said my mum. "You stay there! I'll show the sergeant out."

She led Sergeant Todd out into the hall and had just opened the front door...

...when Fiona screamed.

CHAPTER 8

STITCHING

Sergeant Todd was bounding up the stairs before we could stop him. My mum and I chased after him.

"Is everything alright?" he shouted, hammering on the bathroom door.

There was a pause.

"Who's that?" asked Fiona.

"Sergeant Todd," the officer replied. "I heard you scream."

"Oh, yes..." said Fiona. "Sorry about that. I, er... had the bath water a bit too hot."

Sergeant Todd glanced at my mum and me before turning back to the door. "Are you hurt?" he asked. "Do you need an ambulance?"

"No, I'm fine!" Fiona called back. "Just had to add a bit of cold. It's fine now."

"OK, if you're sure..."

My mum led the police officer back down the stairs and, this time, got him out of the house. Then she hurried back up to join me on the landing.

"Fiona!" she said. "What's the matter?"

We heard the door unlock and then it opened to reveal the face of my sister. She was very pale. "I ran Max a bath to warm him up, just like you suggested..." she said. Stepping aside, she let us into the bathroom. We both stopped and stared.

Max was in the bath, still wearing his underpants, but that wasn't the disturbing part.

One of his arms had fallen off.

My mum sighed. "Danny," she said, "go and get my sewing kit again."

CHAPTER 9

SCREAMING

The next few days passed in a bit of a blur. Max was decomposing faster than any of us could have imagined, and my mum was doing the best she could to stitch back on any bits that fell off. It soon became clear that Max had to be kept as cold as possible.

So, his half of our room was converted into a freezer. We bought electric fans to surround Max's bed and filled his duvet cover with buckets of ice. Max didn't seem to mind! He spent all his time propped up on his pillows, playing video games (although he had to have his thumbs stitched back into place more than once). He was having the time of his death!

Then came the day I had to go back to school. I knew it wasn't going to be easy, everyone coming up and saying how sorry they were about Max while I had to pretend to be upset.

By now, the news of Max's body disappearing had made the newspapers, and we'd had to lie to the police again and again. Sergeant Todd had been back to the house to search through Max's possessions to see if there was anything there that might lead the police to the grave robber.

We'd had enough notice to get Max out of the way (he was bundled into my mum's wardrobe), but not enough time to move the ice and fans. So I'd had to lie in Max's bed, freezing my bits off while the sergeant rifled through Max's bedside table. I told him I was rehearsing for a school play set in the Antarctic, and wanted to know what it would feel like to try to survive out in the cold.

He didn't say so, but I'm pretty sure that Sergeant Todd thinks I'm weird.

It was just after lunchtime on that first day back at school when everything went wrong. I was in double maths, trying to concentrate on algebra, when Claire Williams, the girl sitting next to me, screamed.

I followed her gaze to the classroom door and my heart sank. Max was standing there!

"Back to... school..." he wheezed, pressing against his chest. "Home... boring..."

And then his arm fell off again.

Chaos erupted. Pupils ran, screaming, from the room and our maths teacher, Mr Parker, collapsed in a dead faint. Within seconds, word had spread that there was a zombie in the school and the corridors flooded with a mixture of terrified and curious kids.

I grabbed Max's arm (and picked up the detached one), and dragged him out through the fire exit. We half ran, half lurched across the playground outside.

"What are you doing here?" I demanded.

"Want to be... normal..." came the reply.

I glanced over my shoulder. By now, some of the braver kids had grabbed broken chair legs and laptop computers — anything they could use as a weapon — and were chasing after us.

"Yeah," I said. "This is normal!"

As we reached the school gates, a car screeched to a halt in front of us. It was my mum!

"Get in!" shouted Fiona, pushing the door open. I threw Max onto the back seat and dived in after him. My mum floored the accelerator and pulled away just as someone's school bag bounced off the windscreen.

"How did you find us?" I asked.

"Lucky guess," Fiona replied.

"Where are we going?"

"Home," said my mum. "We'll pack a few things and go to stay somewhere else for a while. Somewhere out in the..."

Her voice trailed off as we turned into our street. There was a crowd gathered outside our house, shouting and throwing stones at our windows. I recognised some of the mob as the parents of kids in my school.

"They must have phoned home with the news," I said.

"Look!" cried Fiona, pointing. At the other end of the street, a police car was approaching, its lights flashing and sirens blaring.

"What are we going to do?" I demanded.

"Home..." said Max through his rasping breath.

"We can't go home, Max," my mum explained. "There are people there..."

"No..." hissed Max. "My home..."

Just then, an angry cry went up as someone recognised our car. My mum threw the gears into reverse, swung around, trashed someone's garden fence, and roared off in the direction of the cemetery.

"There's someone following," I said, watching another car force its way through the crowd and give chase.

"Who is it?" asked my mum, glancing in the rearview mirror.

"I don't know," I admitted. "I don't recognise the car."

"Well, let's see if they can keep up!"

Despite my mum breaking every speed limit on the roads, the other car kept up with us until we pulled up in the deserted car park of the cemetery. I jumped out and raised my fists as our pursuer pulled up...

...and then my dad got out of the car.

CHAPTER 10

DIGGING

"It's OK," my dad said. "I'm here to help."

I stared at him. "But you were going to…"

"I was drunk and scared, Danny," he said.

"You called him a monster."

"I was wrong," said my dad. "The only monster was me. Now, we can either stand here and argue about it, or we can do what's best for Max."

I paused, then asked, "What do we do?"

"You and Fiona get shovels."

So, as my sister and I broke into the groundkeeper's shed to look for digging equipment, my dad carefully reached into the back of the car and lifted Max out. I saw my mum squeeze his hand as he cradled his son in his arms.

He laid my twin brother on the grass beside his now re-filled grave and kissed him on the cheek. "My special boy," he whispered.

While my mum stitched Max's arm back in place with the emergency sewing kit she keeps in her glove box, my dad, Fiona and I dug down to Max's coffin. By now, the sun was setting and a cool breeze had started to blow.

The broken pieces of the old coffin lid had been removed, and a new one put in its place. Dad dropped down into the grave to open it.

It started to rain.

Mum helped Max to his feet and he shuffled over to the hole. Dad helped him down and laid him against the soft, white lining. I needn't have worried. It was a perfect fit.

"Goodbye, son," he said softly.

"Goodbye, sweetheart," said my mum, fighting back her tears. "I'll never forget you."

"Bye, stinky bum!" grinned Fiona, crying hard.

Max turned his gaze towards me. I looked down through my tears at my brother. My twin. My best friend.

"See you, buddy," I said.

"Not if... I see... you... first..." hissed Max.

Then he closed his eyes.

Forever.

THE END